www.somethingwickedlyweird.com

To read more about Stanley, look out for all the
Something Wickedly Weird books:

The Wooden Mile
The Icy Hand
The Silver Casket
The Darkling Curse
The Smugglers' Mine
The Treasure Keepers

Read more spooky tales in Dust 'n' Bones,

also by the award-winning Chris Mould.

And visit Chris at his website:
www.chrismouldink.com

## THE TREASURE KEEPERS

# CHRIS MOULD

*Hodder
Children's
Books*

A division of Hachette Children's Books

For Steve, Helen, Jack and Thomas Dighton

Text and illustrations copyright © 2009 Chris Mould

First published in Great Britain in 2009
by Hodder Children's Books

The right of Chris Mould to be identified as the Author and Illustrator
of the Work has been asserted by him in accordance with the
Copyright, Designs and Patents Act 1988.

1

A Catalogue record for this book is available from the British Library

ISBN  978 0 340 95056 2

Printed and bound in Germany by GGP Media GmbH

The paper used in this book is a natural recyclable product made from
wood grown in sustainable forests. The hard coverboard is recycled.

Hodder Children's Books
A division of Hachette Children's Books
338 Euston Road, London NW1 3BH
An Hachette Livre UK company

Admiral Buggles

Crampton Rock

The Clipper

It was later than usual, but Stanley Buggles was being kept awake. The distant howl that sang across the moor was somehow louder tonight. It was a reminder to him that all was not well on the island he had made his home.

His worries rolled around his head all night, until eventually he climbed out of bed and now here he was, seated at the window, staring into

the darkness and recalling all his fears.

Firstly, the sinister figure of escaped
criminal Edmund Darkling, who he knew was
prowling the night in the shape of a wolf.

Secondly, the endless gold mine that ran
like a maze beneath the island itself – and the

thought that one day its secret might be revealed by the grubbiest of hands, the hands of old MacDowell. This craftiest of pirates had managed to convince Stanley and his good friend Daisy Grouse that he had no interest in what might lie beneath the ground. But when they had innocently led him to it, somehow the magical glint of gold under the candlelight had changed his mind.

Right now, Stanley had no idea of the whereabouts of MacDowell. The old buccaneer had left the island in a sailing boat, but it was no great secret that he would be back.

Stanley looked further into the blackness. The glow from the lighthouse drew his eye and he thought of Daisy and her uncle Lionel, the lighthouse keeper. Daisy would be tucked up in bed right now, safe from harm.

But trouble was brewing and Stanley knew that young Miss Grouse would be his greatest help in the times ahead.

He could see a figure in the nearest watchtower. It was the night watchman, draped in a blanket and no doubt wrapped in a wind-blown slumber. This was not uncommon. By now the drink would have got the better of him, and the last thing on his mind would be watching out for the wolf. Everyone knew that it took a good bottle of grog just to gather the bravery to sit at the black of night on the look-outs, with only the biting cold to keep you company.

Eventually Stanley also drifted into a slouching sleep that left him propped up in the window like a rag-doll. As the early morning light nudged the harbour awake, he lifted his head again. A hazy outline of something tall was coming into view. Stanley rubbed his eyes and stretched his aching bones.

It was a ship, and not just any old ship. It must have had a hundred sails. A clipper ship, long and narrow with white sails waving like carnival flags. And it was heading into the welcoming shape of Crampton Rock harbour.

Stanley watched the vessel roll into the bay, and someone heading along the harbour wall. It was Mr Grouse, Daisy's uncle. His tall shape was unmistakeable. He waved at the ship as it steered to a safe spot and dropped anchor.

On board, three men let a small boat down into the water and after climbing in they made their way to the harbour wall.

Stanley kept watch. He knew by now that they would be traders. Penelope Spoonbill,

the Mayoress,
appeared from
the village square.
With a coat wrapped
around her nightclothes
she rushed to the shore and
greeted the sailors along with Mr Grouse.
They handed her a box of some kind,

15

perhaps a gift, shook hands like old friends and headed into the village.

But Stanley could see something else from where he sat. Back on board the ship a long, thin shape was shifting around. Someone else was there, someone who had opted not to leave the vessel and greet the villagers. Someone who slunk around in the background, preferring to stay unnoticed. Maybe he had work to do on board and would join them later.

Maybe so, thought Stanley … And maybe not!

After Stanley had coaxed himself back to life and decorated his bony frame with the clothes that lay scattered around his room, he went downstairs. On his way to the kitchen he wandered over to the glass case

where
his old friend
the pike lived.

'And how are you?' he
asked with still-sleepy eyes, dusting the
glass to clear his view.

'Yes, yes, quite well, thank you, Stanley.
Now I can see clearly, there is something I
must tell you,' answered the pike. It was a
rare occasion: he had decided to speak.
There were not many days when he opened
his mouth, but today was one such day.

'Ah, good,' replied Stanley, surprised to
find the pike so approachable at such an
early hour. 'You know I always appreciate
your advice. You've saved me from many a

foul deed in the past.'

'Well. I am old and wise, Stanley, it is true. And I don't dish out my visionary foresight to just anyone. I hope you realize you are in a most privileged position!'

'Yes, I know, so you keep saying. Anyway, can you get on with it? My stomach's rumbling.'

'Of course, my friend. You have a right to know when my view is clouded with ill doings.'

'Ill doings? What ill doings are these?' asked Stanley.

'Hang on,' said the pike. 'It's gone! Sorry. It was right there under my snout and now it's gone.'

Stanley began to walk away. 'Useless old haddock,' he mumbled.

'Wait. I have it. I have it!' The pike paused a moment. 'Ah yes, that is it. Take heed, Stanley. I must warn you not to bring the four-legged one into the house. He will bring you trouble. He has already let you down.'

'The four-legged one? You mean Steadman, the Darkling dog? What else would come here with four legs? Why has he let me down?'

Stanley couldn't understand it. Perhaps the pike meant Mr Darkling, in the form of a wolf? But that made no sense either.

But the big fish would not say any more.

And as Stanley knew, that would be the end of it until he worked things out for himself and more than likely, by then it would be too late.

A cry for Help

Stanley was eager to find out more about the man on board the ship. He hung around in the harbour, hoping he would meet the traders and open a conversation that would answer his questions.

Something flapped in the wind. It was the old 'Wanted' poster of Edmund Darkling, still nailed to a post and so weather-beaten that it was barely recognizable. Poor Mr Darkling. Despite his sinister background, Stanley felt sorry for him: he knew that he longed to be back to normal, at home with his family in the village.

But a stint in the local prison had driven Mr Darkling almost to madness, and by means of escape he had summoned the werewolf curse. This beastly form had allowed him to

WANTED
EDMUND DARKLING

force through the iron bars and now he wandered alone, in hiding, upon the moor.

And Mrs Darkling was responsible for bringing up the Darkling children by herself: no easy task with three strong-willed youngsters.

But Stanley had grown friendly with the Darkling children. The young twins Olive and Berkeley and their older sister Annabelle formed part of the Secret-Keepers Alliance, along with Stanley and, who could forget, Stanley's oldest friend Daisy. They were the only ones on the Rock who knew of the gold mines that rippled beneath their feet. For the rest of their days they knew they must keep the secret held tight.

That night, something sinister pulled Stanley's thoughts away from the smugglers'

23

mine and the mystery man who still sat aboard the clipper ship.

There was a terrible scream out on the moor, a piercing whining moan of someone or something in pain. Ghastly squealing awoke the whole village, but there was not a chance that anyone would venture out at that hour. They would light their candles and peer through their ragged curtains, but none would go there. A lone watchman pointed his flaming torch towards the moor. He shivered and shook so much that the flame almost flickered out, but he could see nothing.

At dawn, a crowd of villagers assembled. They had all heard it, and they knew it spelled something bad. They took to the hills and began searching in their droves. Waves of villagers trickled across the plains like as many ants in their nest.

The alliance assembled too. Stanley and Daisy stood at the fountain in the square, and shortly they were joined by the Darkling children, who had all awoken in the night.

Annabelle was close to tears. She confided in Stanley and Daisy. 'What if something happened to Father in the night? I fear for his safety.'

'In whatever form he takes, Mister Darkling can look after himself. Don't worry. Come on, let's go,' said Stanley – and the Secret-Keepers Alliance marched, business-like, up the grassy climb.

The moor was teeming with villagers, most armed with pitchforks and clubs or broom handles, and many other things that would prove to be useless should they be needed.

The search filled the day, but proved to be fruitless. Not a thing was found. Perhaps some young animal had been taken by the wolf, a badger or fox? The children hung around on the moor, chased through the hills and climbed the rocks until the sky had almost emptied out of all light.

And as they turned home, something happened to make sense of the day's dilemma. A weak noise drifted down to Berkeley, who was hiding from the others under the shadow of a large stone.

'Berkeley,' came a whispering voice. He
looked around and saw nothing.

'Berkeley.' It came again, almost as if it was
trying harder, but couldn't manage it.

Somehow it was coming from above his
head. Berkeley looked up, and atop the large
rock were the fingertips of a mystery figure.

'Come quickly,' squealed Berkeley to the others. Immediately his assistants arrived.

'What is it?' asked Daisy. 'What's wrong?'

'There *is* someone, up … there,' he said, almost doubting himself.

And then an ugly, long-nosed face leered over and steered its eyes down at them.

'Hi kids!' came a croaky, pathetic voice, as a huge hat pulled a shadow over their faces.

'Mac!' they all shouted in disbelief. And sure enough, it was old MacDowell, the pirate who had betrayed them by taking gold from the mines. His scrawny shape began to slide down from the rock, and he landed in a crumpled mess at their feet, blood caked all over him. A smash of glass resounded and his coat fell open to reveal a hoard of broken bottles. He smelt terrible and whisky was on his breath.

'I'm sorry, lad,' he said in a slurred voice. 'I spent all mi gold. I only came back for a few nuggets more. Yer know, just to get me by, like.'

'What on earth happened to you?' asked Daisy. 'Why were you on top of that rock?'

'I can't remember, lassie,' he admitted, trying to haul himself up. 'I can't remember anythin'. I think I drank too much o' the grog an' whisky, to numb the pain. Aooooh, mi leg.'

'I think that was the pathetic cry we heard in the night,' said Stanley reassuringly. 'We can't leave him like this. Let's take him back to the Hall.'

'Kind as your housekeeper is, Stanley, I don't think he'd ever make it through the door. I'm sure Mrs Carelli will hit the roof if she sees he has returned!' Daisy insisted.

'But look at him,' said Stanley. 'He'll die out here if we leave him.'

They struggled to lift him, even between the five of them. It wasn't so much the weight as the sheer awkward gangling shape of him: he was all arms and legs spilling out like an overgrown rag-doll. Every time they picked one bit up, another limb popped out somewhere else. His right leg had been bleeding profusely.

'I'll get Steadman,' said Annabelle.

'No, please,' begged MacDowell. 'Not the dog.'

But it was too late. Annabelle gave out a strange howling cry and the black silhouette of Steadman came bounding over the moor to their side. He had taken a liking to MacDowell previously and now he was excited to see him back, licking the blood from his hands and face.

It was a sight to behold. Old MacDowell, all washed out and withered, was carried along on the bony spine of Steadman with his arms and legs trailing here and there and the children following on behind.

Mrs Carelli had watched them coming across the moor, so she was hardly surprised to see them arrive and she had just about guessed that the pathetic figure would be MacDowell.

She had held her disapproving expression for the last five minutes as she stood in wait. So as they rounded the corner she was already there with the door open and the confrontation had started before Stanley could muster up an excuse or have any thought of what he might say.

'And where do you think you're taking that long-legged lummox now, Stanley?' she asked. There were five of them of course, as well as the dog, but it was Stanley who was getting the hard words.

'Please, Mrs Carelli. Mister MacDowell is ill. He needs a bed,' pleaded Olive.

'And he deserves a good hiding,' the housekeeper replied.

'Would you like *us* to do it?' asked Berkeley.

Now Mrs Carelli was no great fan of the Darkling children, but she had to admit she was warming to them. They were constantly at the door asking for Stanley and they were well mannered, if nothing else. And now, for the first time, Berkeley had placed a smile on her face.

'Put him back in his room, Stanley,' she ordered abruptly. It was the one he had stayed in previously, before he had shown his true colours. 'And when he's pulled himself together, he'll have to leave. Do you hear me?'

'Oh thank you, Violet,' croaked MacDowell pathetically. 'I'll make it up to yer.'

'And don't you dare call me Violet. It's Mrs Carelli to you and it'll stay that way. It looks like the drink is all that's wrong with him,' she suggested, turning to Stanley, 'save for a few cuts and bruises. Throw him in a warm bath. He stinks to high heaven!'

The children dragged MacDowell from Steadman's back and as he oooh'd and arrghhh'd they carried him through the house and cleaned him up.

A drastic change

Stanley suddenly became aware that he had taken on more than he could manage. Mrs Carelli had said that if he wanted to bring Mac into his own house there was nothing she could do about it, but she wouldn't cook him a meal or make him a drink, nor would she clean his room or attend to any of his needs. Her husband Victor had taken the same stance. They wanted to show their disapproval of the way MacDowell had accepted their hospitality, and then just left like that without so much as a goodbye. 'Disgusting!' Mrs Carelli had said.

So now Stanley was spending his time looking after the very man who had let him down, and Mac showed no signs of improving.

At first he had only a bad cut on his leg and, save for a few scratches and bruises and a fearsome hangover, he was on the mend. But he was going downhill. A fever grew upon him in the night, and he had a putrid yellowness about his skin. That and the foul stink around him were about as much as Stanley could take. He tried to enlist the help of the others, but even the Darkling children couldn't bear the smell, and that was saying something.

Mrs Carelli had taken a look, but her

suggestion of tying Mac to a raft and putting him out to sea was unfair in Stanley's eyes.

Despite all this, one thing was improving. MacDowell's memory!

'Sufferin' shark steaks, I remember now!' he shivered. He was recalling the night out on the moor, with a cup in his hand that shook until the water had emptied out completely. Sweat ran down his brow and only short sentences would come out between panting breaths.

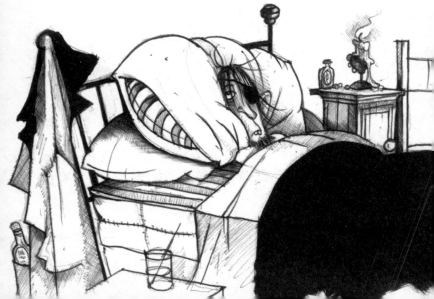

'I was out on the hilltops … Lookin' for
the big rock … The one we rolled over the
exit from the mines … I thought I might
move it … Yer know, to dig out a few chunks
o' the gold an' replenish mi purse, as it were
… Anyway, it was dark … And I was worse
for the drink, yer know … But take a look at
mi leg afore I tell yer the next bit,' he
insisted.

Stanley pulled back the covers. Mac's legs
looked terrible at the best of times. They
were horribly scrawny and at his healthiest
you could almost see the bone through the
skin. Stanley pulled back the dressing. The
wound looked ghastly: the skin had turned
purplish-blue and it didn't look like it wanted
to heal.

'That's a bad cut, Mac,'
said Stanley. 'Does it hurt?'

"Tain't no cut, young Buggles,' MacDowell managed. "Tis a bite … A great big bite.'

And then he dropped his drink and sank further back into his pillow, descending into another sweat-ridden sleep.

Well, that sent Stanley's mind stirring into a mad array of 'what if's! He covered Mac back up and left the room, snuffing out his candle as he went.

When he lay in bed that night he couldn't help thinking that if Mac were to pass away in the night it might be the best thing that could happen! The secret of the gold mines would be safe for ever. MacDowell was the only one of the Secret-Keepers Alliance that Stanley knew he couldn't trust. Taking a clutch of gold and disappearing was a betrayal, the worst thing MacDowell could have done. But he'd done it and here he was, returning for more. Maybe Mac's demise was the best possible way out.

Stanley didn't like the thoughts he was having but nonetheless, he couldn't help having them.

But the night brought further mystery and intrigue.

It must have been one or two in the morning when Stanley was awoken from his slumber. It wasn't the howling out upon the moor or thoughts of what might come that stirred him, it was something closer. Someone was stirring in pain.

'Mac,' said Stanley, and he leapt to his feet to slip into the nearby room.

But instead of being in bed, Mac was on his feet. He stood in moonlit darkness with a poisonous look on his face, breathing heavily.

'Stanley,
god 'elp mi, lad.
Somethin's 'appenin'!'

He dropped to the floor
and the cracking of his bones
awoke the house.

'I think the seafood's disagreed wi' me!' he
squealed, as more cracking came. It was even
louder now and Stanley watched in terrified
disbelief as old MacDowell began to
transform in front of his very eyes.

His long spindly arms and legs began to
shift, sprouting wiry hair. His spine splintered
upwards into an ugly arc as he dropped to his

knees. His features converted slowly into lupine looks and when it was over, all that was left of MacDowell was the patch over his missing eye.

Stanley reeled in horror. It was all becoming clear. The bite on Mac's leg. The howl upon the moor. MacDowell's nightclothes lay in tatters around his clawed feet and he dribbled and growled a rumbling growl. But surely he wouldn't take a chunk out of Stanley. Not after all he had done for him.

Just then an alarmed Mrs Carelli burst through the door with Victor teetering after her. She screamed a terrible scream, so loud the wolf cowered into its haunches. Victor grabbed Stanley and they ran back out of the room, pulling the door tight and turning the key. Click. It was done.

'What on earth is that, and where on earth did it come from?' squeaked Mrs Carelli, her back against the door.

'It's … Mac,' said Stanley with a shake in his voice and a tremble in his knees. 'It's MacDowell. He's been bitten.

That's why he was ill. That's why his hangover turned into fever. He's been bitten, he's ... a werewolf.'

They all looked at one another. 'MISTER DARKLING!' they all cried at once.

By now the beast was raging around the room in torment. It howled and thrashed around the walls, hurling itself against the door and taking great chunks out of the frame. The floor pounded beneath them and the lamps shook on the walls.

Victor and Stanley held tight to the door, just in case, and Mrs Carelli stood motionless with her face in her hands. Furniture collapsing in splinters around the room resounded down the corridor.

With a move that came out of pure exhaustion the wolf collapsed on the floor in the early hours, panting and dribbling with its long slab of a tongue sticking to the floorboards.

In the morning, after a fitful sleep, they ventured in and found MacDowell, back in his original form, curled up on the floor looking helpless. The whole room was destroyed, every

44

piece of furniture reduced to splinters. The bedding was torn into tiny rags and only the iron bed-frame still stood.

'Well, he was never much of a house guest, Stanley, but this is about as much as I can take. He's got to go,' insisted Mrs Carelli.

'But where?' asked Victor.

'We can't let him out on the streets in this condition. He'll kill someone!' added Stanley.

'He wants locking up. I can't have that … *thing* in here,' she said.

Victor and Mrs Carelli were still reeling from the shock of what they'd seen. They knew only too well the history of the Rock, but still, it was hard to take.

'All right,' said Stanley, 'I agree. He *does* want locking up. But *here*, at the far end of the house, in the rounded tower. That way, he's away from us but we can keep an eye on him.

We can bolt the door and leave him something to feed on, to stop him tearing the place up, but we can't let go of him.'

What dreadful circumstances. No one had thought that it would ever come to this, but it had, and they must deal with it.

'I see now!' said Stanley. He was talking to the pike. 'The four-legged one. You meant MacDowell.'

'Forgive me, Stanley. Often I assume that you know what I know. It is a fault of mine. I don't have many, but I do admit to that one. Perhaps in future you should try to think ahead a little. You could have worked it out, I'm sure.' And the pike drifted back into a dreamy sleep where he hid among the reeds and preyed upon the young perch.

Stanley was feeling annoyed at the pike's

mumblings. What was the point of listening to his predictions if he would only ever speak in riddles? It only made things more complicated.

'Perhaps in future I *will* just work it all out for myself,' moaned Stanley, stomping off towards Mac's room.

'Well, tickle me timbers, I'm feeling much better,' chirped MacDowell. 'I don't need to be locked away. I ain't felt this good in a long while.'

But they wouldn't hear any of it. When Victor had fixed a solid array of bars at the rounded windows of the tower, Mac was hurled into his prison, grappling unsuccessfully with the powerful arms of Mrs Carelli.

He pleaded with her at the door. His yellow eye with its narrowed pupil made her scream and she pushed it shut in his face, locking the bolts.

'Yer not short o' meat yerself there, Mrs Carelli,' MacDowell taunted through the keyhole. 'Maybe I'll make a snack out o' yer yet.'

She tore down the corridor screaming, her arms in the air. 'Victor, Victor, wait for me!'

Complications

The Secret-Keepers Alliance were in the
Hall. All five of them were staring in disbelief
at MacDowell through the keyhole and
listening to Stanley's tale.

'It means that father is alive and well,' said
Annabelle.

'Er … yes … I guess you're right,' said
Stanley.

'You'll need to feed him,' said Olive.

'Raw meat,' added Berkeley. 'It's all he will care for. Just like Steadman.'

'Erm … yes,' said Stanley. 'I know.'

He was thinking of other things. The children needed to see MacDowell and be aware of what had happened, but Stanley wanted them to see something else too. He gathered them all in his room.

'Listen,' he said, 'this is important. You see that clipper ship out there? I'm sure it brings trouble.'

'They're only merchants, Stanley,' insisted Annabelle. 'They have always come here. Plying their trade, exchanging their goods.'

'I'm not so sure,' said Stanley. 'When they first came here I watched them roll into the bay and there were four of them on board.

I've only ever seen three of them in the village. After they arrived MacDowell appeared. He won't admit it, but I swear he came here on that ship. I'm sure he was the fourth man!'

'What does that mean?' asked Berkeley.

'If MacDowell came here with those traders, Berkeley, you can bet that he has struck a deal with them. He has brought them here for one thing only. Gold!'

The others had no choice but to agree that Stanley was right, and so a neat little plan was put into place with the help of milk and home-made biscuits.

First things first. The fact that Mr Darkling, the resident werewolf, was father to most of the alliance meant that the children were immune to his harm and could move freely at night. This would come in handy.

When the daylight had disappeared and MacDowell had been fed, the children gathered sneakily in the shadowed corners of the harbour, avoiding the keen eye of the look-outs from the towers. They crammed into a tiny boat and drifted silently to where the clipper ship swayed and bobbed. By this time the crew were back on board for the night and their voices could be heard, laughing and talking. The alliance paddled slowly and gently, biding their time.

The next bit was trickier. They secured the boat to the ship, then all five of them climbed the slippery anchor chain to get on board. Stanley first, then the twins, with Daisy behind them and Annabelle at the back.

They pulled on the ratlines and hoisted themselves clear, and when they had climbed on to the forecastle deck they hid among the barrels. Berkeley was moaning: someone had stood on his foot. Annabelle's hand slipped over his mouth and squeezed hard. Olive

insisted on bringing her headless doll. It had gone everywhere with her and this was to be no exception.

'I can't help thinking that this would have been easier if it had been just me and you,' whispered Daisy to Stanley.

'True,' he agreed, 'but don't forget the importance of the alliance. We need to stick together. They won't have faith in our plans if they don't see what I think we're all about to see. It will make them realize that

this is for real. Hang in there, Daisy, it's worth
it. Trust me!'

Right now, the crew were down in the
living quarters. The children spilled across
the timbers and assembled around the hatch.
Stanley pulled it back ever so slowly until a
chink of candlelight and the sound of raised
voices announced that the crew were right
there beneath them.

Olive and Berkeley were arguing.

'Shhh,' said Stanley.

'I can't see,' said Olive. 'I want to see.'

Annabelle's hand sprung into action again
and muffled the noise.

'Shut it,' she whispered abruptly.
'You don't need to see, you need to
be quiet.'

'But Stanley wants to show us
something,' Olive mumbled.

Annabelle gave her a look that meant she would say no more.

'What was that?' came a voice from below.

Stanley lowered the hatch back into place, but he could hear that someone was coming up to take a look. Footsteps resounded on the timber staircase.

'Quick,' said Stanley, 'into the barrels.'

The children leapt into action, each of them looking for a spare barrel. Stanley lifted the lid of the last one and hoisted Annabelle in, but as she dropped she found it was full of water.

SPLASH!

The hatch lifted. Stanley watched
Annabelle pull the lid over her barrel, then
threw himself over the side of the ship and
hung on to the ratlines. He was dangling by
his hands and the ropes were rough around
his fingers. He wouldn't last long.

'There's nothing here,' came a voice. 'You're
panicking again. I told you about that. You
make me nervous when you panic.'

Then there was the noise of someone
slipping. 'It's wet here. Why is it wet? What's
going on with this water barrel?'

Stanley was struggling. A numbness came
over his hands, and he couldn't even tell
whether he was holding on or not.

The man peered into the barrel and saw
the thick black hair on top of Annabelle's
head. Through the darkness it looked like

rope. He mumbled to himself. 'Rope in the water barrels. Why 'ave we got rope in the water barrels?'

Then someone called him. 'Come on, we ain't got all night.'

Finally, the man returned to his comrades.

Stanley barely had the strength to haul himself back up. His hands were now red-raw from hanging on.

'Can we be quiet this time?' he whispered. He looked at Annabelle and saw that she was dripping wet and shivering uncontrollably.

'What did you say, Stanley? Erm ... "It's worth it. Trust me"!' said Daisy.

'Please,' he returned. 'Not now.'

But they'd had a stroke of luck. Stanley looked over the forecastle deck to see that the man had returned inside by going down the steps to the main deck and through the

door. He had left it
only slightly open,
but it was enough.

They filed down
the stairs and slipped
inside where they hid
behind a series of
wooden crates, listening
to every word.

Stanley studied the
men's faces and
remembered their
names. There was Mr
Beale, seemingly the head of the
operation. Thin and bandy-legged, almost
like MacDowell, but dandily dressed and
with a narrow menacing look. Then there
was Mr Nook, tall and powerful with jet-
black hair and deep-set eyes. And the third

one was Mr Grimble, short and squat in
shape with a pig-like nose and a balding head
that held on to three wispy uncontrollable
strands of hair.

'Now where were we?' asked Mr Grimble. He kept feeling for his hair and stroking it back into place.

'The missing sailor!' said Mr Nook, looking displeased.

'Ahh yes,' continued Mr Beale, taking over and confirming that he was the one in charge. 'Our advisor. He seems to have gone missing and I can't understand why. He knows we will be paying him a sum of money for his help and information, yet he slipped away into the night and hasn't returned.'

'Perhaps the *werewolf* has taken him?' suggested Mr Grimble, and he and Mr Nook laughed out loud.

'Quite clever though, don't you think,' interrupted Mr Beale. 'The werewolf tale, I mean. It keeps treasure seekers from the island, that's for sure.'

'Well yes, apart from us though,' agreed Mr Grimble. 'But we know better than to believe all that baloney. Anyway, I'm sure we will soon catch up with Mister MacDowell, and then we can get things moving.'

'I ain't taking no risks,' replied Mr Beale. 'I got a tasty-looking rifle at the ready, and I got this as well.' He took a small wallet out of his pocket. Inside was a shining silver bullet. 'Only one way to be rid of a werewolf,' he grinned.

The children stared at each other. Stanley was right, MacDowell *was* part of the crew and what's more, they looked like they were here for the treasure and even Mr Darkling wouldn't get in their way.

'Well I'll be darned! They're no better than pirates!' whispered Daisy.

Olive took her doll in one hand and raised

the other, clenching her fist and shaking it.
'How could he bring those villains here like
that, Daisy?'

'*Shhhh.*'

Annabelle's hand was back again, followed
by the look, followed by silence.

Stanley looked around. The boxes they
hid behind had something written on them.
DANGER – HIGHLY EXPLOSIVE!

'First, of course, we must make sure that
the gold mine exists. We would not wish to
look foolish or go to great lengths for no
reason,' said Beale.

'How do we go about this?' asked Nook.

'By surveying the tunnels. We will access
them through a basement that MacDowell
will lead us to. He has done this several times
already, he claims, and as long as we go at
the right time it will be no problem.'

Stanley had heard enough for now. He knew what they were up to and who was involved.

The next thing was to get back home in one piece. Annabelle was shaking so much with cold and fear that the whole boat was almost rocking.

Like a line of bilge rats they trickled back outside and scuttled over the deck, climbing back on to the huge anchor chain and dropping into the boat. Stanley had to admit that, despite the hiccups, the Darkling children were extremely brave. And their sight in the dark was incredible. But Olive dropped her doll in the water on the way down, and the next five minutes were spent using the boat oars as fishing rods to retrieve the headless toy in her lace and velvet dress.

They returned home through the black of

night and sneaked into their beds. Stanley fell asleep as he listened to the thumping and howling at the far end of the house, wondering what on earth they were going to do next.

The missing sailor

The Secret-Keepers Alliance were holding
another meeting.

It was scheduled to be *'held in secure premises
and with adequate provisions and security'*.

What this actually meant was that it would
be in Stanley's bedroom with large amounts
of biscuits and milk, and Steadman would be
there as a security guard. Stanley had

provided the dog with a bone, but the
Darkling children had a terrible habit of
picking at the raw meat.

'We don't like biscuits!' insisted Olive.

'Or sweet things,' added Berkeley.
Although he had been known to eat sugar
cubes when they were low on uncooked flesh
so actually he was lying.

Everybody threw in their ideas. Some were
good, some were bad and some were just
plain stupid.

'We could just give them the gold and let them pay us for it,' suggested Berkeley, who still hadn't grasped that the prospectors were about to blow the island to smithereens to gain access to the mines.

Stanley explained it all over again.

'Oh yes,' Berkeley said. 'I remember now!'

Annabelle raised her eyebrows, shook her head and decided not to say anything. He was still young. He only understood things when you drilled them into him. And, of course, Olive was the same age, but questioned things a little less. Her mind was often elsewhere.

That was part of the problem with the alliance: some of its younger members had a habit of taking things in the wrong direction. Whether or not Daisy liked Olive's headless doll was not really part of the agenda but it was probable that they had now spent twenty minutes discussing it.

They pushed on.

'Here's my best idea,' said Stanley. 'I can't see any reason why it wouldn't work.'

Everyone leaned their heads in closer, ears pricked up.

'We let MacDowell show the mines to the prospectors.'

'Ooooh no,' said Olive and Berkeley at once.

'Please ... just listen. Listen carefully and wait until I've finished,' said Stanley.

He continued. 'We let MacDowell show the mines to the prospectors because it's the only way to prove to them that there's actually nothing there. Nothing except a maze of old tunnels dug away by the force of the sea, with barnacles and old stones and rock and *nothing else.'*

The others looked confused but nobody spoke. Stanley hadn't finished. He had them hanging by a thread as he stopped to dunk one of Mrs Carelli's prize ginger nut biscuits into his milk before swallowing it whole.

'But here's what we do before we let MacDowell out of his prison to lead them to the mines. There must be a thousand tins of paint down in the scullery. We'll take a tin each and a brush and we'll start painting. We'll put a coat of paint over each and every twinkling nugget of gold until it looks like I just described it. Like nothing. Like rock and stones and sand.'

'But that would take a lifetime,' said Annabelle. 'It's a good idea, but we would be there for ever!'

'You're right, Annie,' said Stanley. 'But we

don't need to paint the whole thing. If they think there's nothing there they won't bother walking right through every tunnel. They'll suspect straight away that they've been tricked if they can't see gold within a hundred steps. I mean let's face it, MacDowell doesn't really look like an honest business man, does he?'

'It's worth a try,' said Daisy. 'I don't think we have anything better!'

'Let's do it,' said Berkeley. He jumped up and knocked a jug of milk all over the dog.

'BERKELEY!'

Stanley had worked out that if they let Mac out to 'do business' it would have to be during the day. At least that meant he was safe from transforming into a wolf whilst he went about his task. They would just need to

make sure he was tucked up in his tower
before dark. The main thing was that Stanley
knew MacDowell would have to make plans
to go down in the daylight.

First things first. Before they collected
their paint stash, Stanley 'accidentally' left
Mac's door open, knowing full well that he
would slip away to meet with his business
colleagues whilst Mrs Carelli was out
shopping in the village.

The Secret-Keepers
Alliance
(decorating
department)
made their
way
around the
back of the
village

through all the short cuts that hid them from view. When they reached the Darkling house, Stanley insisted that the twins should start by painting the front door.

'Why?' said Berkeley. 'I thought we were painting the *tunnels*.'

'Of course we are,' agreed Stanley. 'But in secret. You don't want your mother asking why you're covered in black paint. You're already in a mess and we haven't even taken the lids off the tins yet.'

It took all five of them to lift the stone flag in the basement. Stanley was surprised at how strong the Darkling children were, but even then it was ridiculously heavy.

Whilst the children painted, Stanley couldn't resist running along and sneaking a look down at the harbour. And sure enough, there was Mac. He'd managed to convince

one of the fishermen that they'd be
saving his life if they just took
him out to the clipper ship
in the bay.

Everything was
falling neatly into
place.

Finally, they
thought they'd
painted far

enough in (and it did seem like a long way). If they went any further they probably wouldn't make it back anyway, Stanley decided.

Annabelle organized the clear-up. Everyone accounted for, stone flag down, brushes washed, paint lids back on, hands and faces clean. The tins and brushes were hidden in the basement for now and the children, pleased with their day's work, ran along the beach for half an hour with Steadman bounding alongside.

By this time old MacDowell had left the clipper ship, having made his arrangements. When he saw the children he sneaked out of their way and now he was meandering along the harbour wall, feeling pleased with himself. He was completely unaware that the alliance were only pretending not to see him.

Suddenly something took him by the arm,
a firm grip that felt like a vice.

'And what are you doing out o' your cell,
you long-legged lummox?'

'Ahh, Violet,' he answered, staring back at Mrs Carelli with one weird yellowy eye. 'I had a moment's business to attend to, yer know. A man of my importance can't keep still for long. Life goes on an' all that. Now if you let me go we'll say no more about it.'

She ignored his ramblings and carried him back to the Hall, his feet barely touching the ground. As she did so the children caught sight of the commotion and watched with belly-aching amusement.

'Perfect,' said Stanley. 'Now, he's back in his hole for the night. We'll let him out again tomorrow.'

'Aye, aye, captain,' Daisy said, giving him a salute.

Inside, Mrs Carelli was bunging MacDowell into his room.

'Get your filthy ragged bones in there, you

wily old wolfman,' she bellowed. 'Look at the state of your room, it's filthy and it stinks to high heaven.'

'Please, Mrs Carelli, I'm much better now. Much much, better.'

'You don't look it,' she insisted, bolting the door.

His frustration turned to anger and he aimed his one good eye at the keyhole, watching her wander back down the corridor.

'Now there's a sight and a half,' he shouted. 'There's a good bit o' meat on those buttocks, I'll bet.'

Mrs Carelli placed her hands over her rump and ran as fast as she could down the corridor, screaming.

'I'm sure I'll be hungry tonight, Violet,' Mac shouted after her. 'Will yer be servin' supper, or shall I come an' get it myself? HA

HAAAAAAA,' he roared as she tore down the steps to the kitchen.

'Victor, Victor!'

Finding the way

Twilight returned to Crampton Rock. The children were wrapped up in their beds and out in the bay, the traders sat talking into the night. Only the rush of the sea, as the ship bobbed and swayed in the bay, prevented them from hearing the sinister howls upon the moor.

They poured another drink and said cheers

to their impending success.

'Gentlemen, our fortunes are about to change,' said Mr Beale. 'Tomorrow we will take a look at what promises to leave us very comfortable for the rest of our days.'

The others smiled and raised their glasses. 'We'll drink to that,' they agreed.

Meanwhile, MacDowell was in the middle of one of his turns. He was thrashing around in the tower, tearing chunks out of what was left of the furniture. His skin reddened with the heat that boiled inside him. Masses of thick hair sprouted from him like weeds.

He pawed greedily over the meat and bone that lay scattered around the floor for him, and pulled frantically at the bars and bolts that Victor had secured to the windows. Finally, he fell asleep in a heap.

Mrs Carelli lay in her bed with her heart

thumping. She couldn't take it much longer, she'd told Victor. What on earth would become of old MacDowell? Things could surely not stay as they were for long.

Across the moor, another of his kind prowled and lurked in search of prey.

These were dark days indeed for the Rock. The werewolf brood was expanding and now the island lay in danger of complete extinction.

The following morning, Stanley was alerted by loud shouts from MacDowell's tower.

'Stanley! Stanley Buggles! I need to speak to yer, lad,' came a croaking rattle through the keyhole.

Stanley wanted to ignore Mac, but he grew so tired of the noise that he made his way down to the tower. And, of course, he knew what it was going to be about. MacDowell had made arrangements with his business associates to take a tour around the mines and he wouldn't be doing that unless Stanley let him out.

'Stanley, I got a little proposition for yer,'

Mac began, in his slimiest voice.

'Oh, yes,' said Stanley. 'And what would that be? I'm sure I wouldn't be interested. Is there something in it for me?'

'Well, now I'm a little better, I thought I might just take a stroll in the afternoon sun today. It'll help to bring me back to life, if yer get me meanin'. Per'aps yer'd be kind enough to leave me door ajar, so to speak!'

Stanley knew full well that if he didn't let Mac out their plan would go to waste. But all the same, he wasn't about to give in immediately.

'Now why would I go putting the Rock in danger, Mac?' he started. 'You've already done enough of that yourself. I'm a touch more careful than you are, you should know that by now. I think perhaps you're better off right where you are, don't you?'

Mac grew desperate. If he didn't make his appointment, the traders were likely to give up on him. He'd already had their boat swimming in the harbour for longer than they'd planned.

'Stanley, pleeeeaaaaase,' he begged. His face came closer to the keyhole and his sniffling long beak almost poked right through it. 'I'm beggin' yer, lad. Just a stroll. Just for an hour.' By now he was almost in tears.

'I'll think about it,' said Stanley in his best, most unconcerned voice, and then he walked off down the corridor leaving Mac not knowing what he was going to do.

Meanwhile, the Darkling children were sitting with their mother at the kitchen table. They needed to ensure that the house would be empty when MacDowell and Co. came to look at the mines.

'Mother, you need some fresh air,' insisted
Annabelle. 'Why don't we take a walk in the
sunshine this afternoon? Across the moor, just
us. We could take Steadman. We'll take a
picnic basket, there's that big bone we picked
up from the butcher's.'

'But what will the dog have to eat?' asked
Mrs Darkling.

'Mother, the bone is for the dog!'
Annabelle returned.

Mrs Darkling was not
herself, not by a long
way. Since Mr Darkling
had been put in
prison, and especially
since he had escaped, she
had grown weak and listless.
Where once she had been strong

and opinionated now she was dismissive and showed a lack of care for almost everything around her. To Annabelle, it seemed as if *they* were looking after *her*.

By mid-afternoon, everything was beginning to happen. The only downside was that the weather was not as good as they had all hoped. Mrs Darkling could not understand why the children were so keen to walk in the rain, and MacDowell's excuse of taking in the sunshine was looking more than a little weak.

Stanley had 'accidentally' unlocked Mac's door and sent him out

through the kitchen. He'd warned
MacDowell that if he was caught by Mrs
Carelli, he mustn't mention Stanley.

'Aye, aye, Stanley. Mum's the word.'

Mrs Darkling and the children ventured
out on to the moor with a picnic basket and
an umbrella.

And three men came ashore
from their ship to make

'arrangements' with a colleague!

Stanley and Daisy were the only ones left with nothing to do. They ventured up into the lighthouse and watched what they could as events unfolded.

The Darkling family were playing in the puddles on the moor. The sinister shapes of MacDowell and Co. lurked near the Darkling house.

Stanley continued to eye the movements of MacDowell and his sinister company. They wheedled around the back of the house until they were out of sight, but he knew what their movements would be. They would head into the mines in the only possible way, sliding down the coal chute into the cellar, lifting up the flagstone and creeping into the hole.

'Very soon, Daisy, they'll be very

disappointed by what they find,' Stanley assured her.

'I hope so,' Daisy said, her fingers crossed.

'You had better not be leading us on some merry dance, MacDowell,' said a snake-eyed Mr Beale as they stood hunched together in the cramped cellar waiting for Mr Nook to use his muscle and lift the stone flag.

But within the next half an hour an argument began to unfold. It indicated a perfectly executed plan.

'Mister MacDowell,' began the captain, 'you've brought us all the way down here and we can only see grit and sand and rock. I agree, the tunnels are impressive. I think perhaps you imagined how fantastic they would look festooned in gold. But you're wasting our time here.'

'But it was 'ere, I swear. It was
everywhere. It was in the rock itself, I know it
was! Per'aps a little further.' MacDowell held
out a welcoming hand, leading them deeper.
Maybe those kids have been at it, he
thought, picking away now and then, taking
a little at a time. And then there was the stash
that he'd taken for himself, a considerable
amount, if he was honest.

He pushed them on around the next
corner. But still it remained the same:
blackened rock caked in dirt and seaweed and
a salty smell that they couldn't stomach.

'I've seen enough,' said Mr Beale. 'There
ain't no gold here. There ain't nothing, except
a trail o' tunnels and too much salt an'
barnacles. Come on, we've wasted enough
time.'

They began to leave, ignoring
MacDowell's pleas. But when Mr Beale and
Mr Nook climbed out, they noticed that Mr
Grimble was missing. They returned to the
hole. Mr Grimble was deeper inside, more

inquisitive than the other two. The tunnels were like nothing he'd ever seen, embedded with skeletal figures from centuries gone by.

'Mister Grimble, are you there?'

'Won't be long,' he shouted, and his voice came echoing back along the narrow walkways.

He found every turn fascinating. Fantastic shapes, worn away by the never-ending swirling rinse of the salty water. He kept ignoring his friends' calls, trapped by his compulsion.

And then he turned and looked back. Was it the tunnel on the left he had just come through, or the one on the right?

The way had opened out into a small cave, and now all the openings looked the same.

'This one,' he said to himself. 'I'm sure of it.' And, spooked by his moment of

confusion, he decided he would head back.
'Here I am,' he called.

But then he stopped again and looked up
as something caught his eye, twinkling in the
dark. He ran his hands over the rock, staring
harder through the dim light of his candle.

Gold! He was sure of it. Nothing less than
pure gold.

His heart beat faster. It was true! It *was*
here. And it was everywhere. Suddenly his
eyes woke up to what lay smiling back at him
from the curved sides of the tunnels. Shining,
glistening, gorgeous gold. He raced around,
running his hands over the walls in
excitement, backwards and forwards,
laughing to himself.

He shouted out. 'It's here. I've found it!'

Back at the entrance, Beale and Nook
stared at each other. They could hear a

muffled noise from somewhere, but now it was further away. *Much* further away.

Grimble turned to head back in excitement. But was it this passage, or that one? No hang on, it was neither of those. It was the one over here. Wasn't it?

Then a noise. A noise he'd been able to hear all along, but that had grown closer. It was the rush of the sea. Ahead of him, a swirling trickle of salty wash poured into a waiting hole and formed a small pool.

And behind it, there was more. Much more.

# 7

## A gem of an idea

Suddenly, Grimble's tactics needed to change. He had gone from 'fascinated explorer' to 'trapped desperado' in one short step.

Back in the basement the sound of his calls grew more and more muffled. Mac tried to head towards him through the tunnels, but he heard the rush of the sea and watched the water seeping in, and that was enough. He

fled. He still had
nightmares about
escaping the
water.

'Head upwards
and dig away above
you when you get as high
as you can go.' MacDowell cried.
His voice echoed unheard through the
curved and craggy passages.

They had to leave Grimble. They could
see that, very quickly, the water was taking
control of the mines. No one could argue
with the might of the sea.

Outside, an argument spilled into the
square. Beale and Nook berated MacDowell:
the mines were empty, and they'd left a good
colleague to find his way out of a watery
prison. If he didn't appear out on the moor as

Mac had promised he would, they'd be less than happy.

They wandered up to the moor, searching and calling, as MacDowell stood panicking in the village square.

Stanley and Daisy saw their opportunity and moved in. They had watched the men emerging and seen that one of them was missing. It appeared that their plan had worked, but still they felt terrible. They knew how it felt to be trapped down in the mine.

'I think perhaps you'd better get yourself back in your kennel,' joked Daisy. 'It's growing dark. We don't want any nonsense now, do we?'

'I'll come quietly,' said Mac. He was definitely down in the dumps. He stared across the moor, hoping to catch a glimpse of three men.

But there was nothing.

Below their very feet, Grimble was searching desperately, perspiring at the thought that he might never see the daylight again, clambering hopelessly through the dark with a feeble candle that was almost burned out.

Trickles and gushes seeped in everywhere. 'Upwards,' he said to himself, trying to cheer himself up. 'Upwards and onwards.' He hadn't heard a word of MacDowell's advice, but it made sense to head up. The higher the better.

And then a stroke of luck presented itself. Grimble heard a sound: chirping and whistling, in short sharp shrills. It was a bird! In the caves? That

meant only one thing. Nearby was a way out. However small it was, it would do, he thought.

Grimble followed the sound and a moment later he caught sight of something small, flitting around in the darkness. Grey and black and white it was, hopping among the stones and bobbing and dipping in the shallow pools of water. And there was a faint chink of light! The gold still shone around Grimble, but his interest in survival had taken over and somehow its glow was less now than before.

He stumbled and tripped and startled the

little creature, which darted forward and swooped out through the hole.

It was only a small opening, but Grimble was able to push and pull himself out. He was free, on a short ledge in a precarious position high out on the cliff face at the north-west corner of the Rock. He would have to climb. It would take a while and it would not be easy.

The sun had sunk to the horizon by the time a pair of hands appeared at the very edge of the moor. They felt their way among the foliage and clutched at stalks and branches, before the rest of Mr Grimble appeared, red-faced and panting, pulling himself up.

All he had to do now was walk across the island back to the harbour, and he could tell his colleagues that it had all been very much worthwhile.

Simple.

Well, simple except for one thing. To make your way across a moor at dusk would be a pleasant walk in many parts of the world. But here, of course, such a task involved a certain risk. A risk not yet taken seriously by Grimble and his friends.

A pair of yellowy eyes peered down from above. They were just awakening. Edmund Darkling had made his nightly transformation. He had shed his malnourished human form and become the four-legged menace that kept Crampton Rock in a state of high alert.

It lurked among the tall grass that blew in waves around the hills.

Grimble began to walk, shakily, across the moor.

He was being watched.

From the harbour, a horn blew and one of the look-outs shouted to Nook and Beale. It was past the hour of dusk and they must get indoors.

The wolf chose its moment, leaping at its victim with bared teeth. Grimble's arms and legs flew out. He screamed and the wolf howled in response, jaws open, teeth bared. Biting and tussling prevailed and blood began to flow.

But right then Beale's shotgun blasted, drowning out every other possible noise. He had missed, but the beast was startled and darted off into the blackness, leaving a sore and wounded Grimble. A trail of spilled blood petered out into the dark.

The three colleagues made haste back to their ship. Grimble did not yet have the energy to tell his friends of the treasure that awaited in the mines. He tried but, through

his exhaustion, the words just wouldn't come.
And they had already planned to set sail the
next day.

Next morning, the
Darkling children
joined Stanley
and Daisy
at the
Hall.
They were
discussing the
previous day, and of
course sniffing around Mrs Carelli's baking at
the same time.

Berkeley and Olive were keen to tell Mrs
Carelli of the plans they had to cure
MacDowell. They were going to feed him to
Steadman limb by limb. She liked that idea!

Stanley and Daisy were locked in deep conversation at the kitchen table, whispering furiously about what to do next, and how to do it.

Annabelle ambled down the kitchen corridor, taking in the paintings and looking at the strange objects. She felt at home.

'A fine collection, wouldn't you agree, Annabelle? There's so much more to it than first meets the eye,' came a voice.

She looked over her shoulder. There was no one there. She looked all around, up and down. She was alone, and frightened.

'Forgive me, young Darkling, I do not wish to startle you, merely to make you aware of my presence. Your assistance is needed.'

The voice seemed to come from behind her, but when she turned to look there was just an old glass case with a stuffed pike

inside it. She looked again. Its eye had
shifted. She was sure of it.

'That's right,' the voice carried on, and by
now she was sure it came from the crusty old
fish. 'You take a good look. I'm not as young

and handsome as I used to be, but there's no need to look so appalled.'

'I'm ... sorry,' gasped Annabelle.

'Now listen here, young lady. The lad has neglected to seek my advice. I think perhaps I upset him, and now he punishes me by turning a blind eye. I fear he is about to celebrate a victory that hasn't yet been won.'

'*What?*' said Annabelle.

'Oh, not you as well,' the pike moaned. 'The word is PARDON!'

'I'm sorry ... pardon,' Annabelle said ... but that was the end of it. She tried and tried but he would say no more.

Annabelle stayed quiet for the rest of the day. Perhaps she had dreamed it. Maybe she was going mad. Or could it be that she really *had* heard the pike?

Stranger things have happened upon this

island, she thought to herself, but she kept the secret of the underwater speaker to herself.

Meanwhile, the clipper ship had readied its sails and was about to lift anchor. MacDowell watched from a peephole in his barred-up windows. He'd seen the sails open up like white clouds against the blue of a perfect late afternoon.

'No,' he winced, staring with his one eye through the gap. 'Don't go!'

Grimble sat up in his bed. He was feeling slightly better: though he felt as if he had a fever coming on, he

was at least able to talk.

He struggled to the door. 'The ship's moving. Why are we moving?'

'Mister Grimble, what are you doing out of your bed?' asked Mr Nook.

'Just drop that anchor, will yer. We're not goin' anywhere just yet. Come inside.'

They sat down at the table and he began to tell his tale. 'Are you trying to tell me I was attacked by a wolf?'

'We don't know what it was. It was dark. Too dark to see at all, really.'

'I don't believe in werewolves and fanciful tales of things in the night. But whatever that crazed animal was it took a right chunk out o' me, I can tell yer,' moaned Grimble. 'It was probably that big black dog that belongs to those kids in the village.'

His eyes were yellowing and his skin

looked pasty. 'Those caves have given me a
fever,' he insisted. 'But I'll be up and around
and ready for the dig in no time.' And he told
them of the shining golden prize in the
mines.

'It looks like we're staying then,' said Beale.

'Aye, aye, captain,' said Nook. 'Time to put
phase two of our plan into action.'

Beneath
the
Rock

It was Daisy who heard it first, from her uncle at the lighthouse. The traders were buying an old property on the island. Their application to become residents had been accepted by the local committee. What with their good links in the trading world and their history of trading with the Rock in the past, they would be a credit to the island.

'*What?*' said Stanley at the top of his voice. 'Does the Mayoress have any idea what they're really here for? They're about to blow this place to smithereens.'

'Well, of course she doesn't,' said Daisy. 'And how on earth do we tell her? We already know we can't let the information out, not to anyone.'

'Yes, Daisy, you're right. Despite people's best intentions, we all know what happens to secrets!' Stanley agreed.

'What happens to secrets, Stanley?' asked Berkeley, who sat listening.

'Secrets, Berkeley, are what grown-ups pass on to one another, one person at a time,' Stanley said. 'And that just isn't good enough. Our secret has to remain a secret. It must never go outside the circle.'

'All right,' said Berkeley.

But it left them without a single cause for opposition to the idea of Beale, Nook and Grimble taking up an old mill house that had stood empty for some time.

'Don't worry,' said Stanley, addressing his troops. 'We'll dig deep and find a way.'

'What's happening?' MacDowell begged Stanley through his keyhole. He was desperate to know, but he had questions he daren't ask. Why was the ship still here? What had happened to Grimble? Had he made it home again?

MacDowell was going stir-crazy in his wolf pen. And with all this time on his hands, he was beginning to plot his escape.

It seemed like no time at all had passed before the traders were a part of the village

community. The old mill house sat crookedly among the rest of the buildings in the village. It was across the cobbled street and further down than the old Darkling place, just a short step from Victor's candle shop.

The children watched helplessly as they saw them bring boxes of belongings into the old house. Boxes that they knew contained, among other things, explosives. Something told them that their plan had not gone as perfectly as they had wished. And why were there three of them again? What had happened to Mr Grimble? He seemed less than capable, as if he was ill, but he insisted on joining in.

'Take a rest,' his colleagues told him. 'You're sweating like mad.'

His skin had yellowed and his eyes had

sunk back into his skull, leaving dark
shadows around the sockets.

At the end of a long day, the children hung
around outside the house and listened
curiously. Berkeley was all ears. In fact, all the
Darkling children were the same: they could
hear more than the average person, for sure.
'Heightened senses', Mrs Carelli called it.
And she was right.

Chink … chink … chink.

'Come on, Stanley, surely you can hear it,'
laughed Berkeley.

'No, I can't,' Stanley said, pressing his ear
against the wall. 'Not at all. But I'd like to
know what it is. Is he kidding me?' he asked
Annabelle.

'No,' she insisted. 'I can hear it from here.'

'So can I,' said Olive.

'All right,' Stanley said. 'Then I think they're digging.'

'We need to stop them,' urged Daisy. 'They'll bring the whole place crumbling down if they carry on.'

Olive began to cry.

'No, it's all right, Olive. Not now, it won't happen immediately. But eventually that's what will happen, unless we stop it!'

When they'd calmed Olive down, they decided to head into the Darkling basement. It was growing late and the water was already rising, but it was important to find out what they could. Stanley suggested that the younger ones should go into the house, but there was so much objection that it was easier to let them follow. Off they went in descending size order, with the little ones in tow and the headless doll trailing behind.

Soon they were in the depths of the mines, and now the noise was loud and clear.

CHINK … CHINK … CHINK.

The alliance drew closer, holding their candles out in front and looking expectantly into the dark. The way ahead had changed, been made wider. It sounded as if bodies were milling around in the distance.

'Oh my goodness!' said Daisy, in a voice that could not help itself from raising its volume.

'What is it?' the others asked. They followed Daisy's wide-eyed stare upwards and saw that a huge hole had been dug from the mill house directly into the mines. They could see right up into the main room of the house where the floor had been simply ripped open by the digging. It was wide and gaping and blatant, like a huge cavernous mouth, waiting to swallow up every bit of twinkling gold.

Before they had realized it, footsteps were coming up behind them. They froze in panic, staring at one another.

It was too late to do anything at all.

'Stop right there,' came a voice. The children turned around and before them stood Mr Nook. 'Listen up, lads, we got visitors,' he cried out. The workers stopped and came to join him.

'Well, well, well ... it's those nosy little kids from the 'arbour,' said Beale.

'Came in through the basement, did we? Well listen here, from now on you ain't goin' nowhere.'

He pointed towards them with his gun, and moved forward. 'I got a tasty little silver bullet in here with that wolf's name on it, but if yer'd rather it came whistlin' your way, it's fine by me.'

The children backed into a huddle, stumbling over the rocks and holding on to each other.

Just then something could be heard coming down one of the tunnels. A thundering thump of feet, then a massive roar. The fearsome shape of the wolf emerged and stopped right in

front of the
children,
standing
between them
and the gun.

Beale's hands
began to shake. He lifted the shotgun
but his aim was all over the place. The
sight shook and wouldn't point where he
wanted it to. His fingers trembled on the
trigger.

'No, not Father,' screamed Olive.

BANG. More by luck than judgement the
bullet hit square-on as the lupine form of Mr
Darkling leapt instinctively at the gun.

A single shot. The noise echoed so loud
through the tunnels the whole place shook,
and rock came racing down around them.
Clouds of dust billowed into the air.

When the haze cleared, the form of Edmund Darkling stood right there: one shot with a silver bullet had shaken off the werewolf curse. For a brief moment that felt like forever, they were motionless in surprise. Mr Darkling looked around him, dazed, but he knew that he must come to his senses, and quickly.

'Come, children. Away from here,' he urged. He pushed and tugged them unceremoniously through a small gap in the rock, leaving the shocked traders who had shown themselves to be the worst of pirates.

Soon they were out on the moor, and the children hugged Mr Darkling and cried. They had missed

him so much: it was months now since they
had held him tight and said goodbye to him
in his lonely cell.

They stared at him through the growing
darkness. He was so different – cleaner and
younger-looking, fresher somehow. A terrible
scar was planted in the middle of his forehead.

'But Father, Mother will never believe it is you,' said Annabelle.

'Then I will need your help in convincing her,' he smiled.

'Let's get you home, Father,' suggested Berkeley.

'Yes,' said Mr Darkling. 'I am looking forward to seeing your mother.'

### A terrible sight

Mac was rubbing his hands. As far as he was concerned, his plan was perfect. In next to no time he would be exchanging handshakes and a large purse of money with the traders. Not only had he found a way to escape, but through the peephole in his barred window he had seen the following:

Firstly, the ship was still in the harbour,

and that meant the miners had struck gold.

Secondly, he had spotted all three of them, which put his mind at rest. He now knew for sure that Grimble had made it through the mines and back across the moor.

Now to the escape plan.

Well, to be honest, you couldn't really call it that. It was more of an act of desperation brought on by the fear of losing out completely on his money. He had ripped away the doorframe around the lock. He'd also taken half the wall with it but ah, well. What did he care? Once he had his money he'd be disappearing quickly.

The next part required rather more effort and concentration.

He waited until he thought the house would be empty so that he could sneak out, then slid across the polished floors, snake-like, and ready to roll sideways into an empty room should the need arise. His long nose sniffed the air for human life. (The werewolf curse had its advantages!)

There was nobody around.

The back door through the kitchen would be best, then over the moor to escape into the village and back round, down to the harbour.

So far all was going well.

Until now.

The kitchen door was locked, which he'd expected, but when he climbed out through the kitchen window he realized that Victor was happily tilling the soil in the garden.

'Ahh, crabsticks,' said Mac to himself. 'I'll 'ave to go out through the front.'

But as he trod back down the corridor, Mrs Carelli was just appearing through the front door, arms loaded. He hid himself inside the coat stand. She waddled past him with bags of this and that ... and she'd left the key in the door.

He slunk along the corridor.

A pair of eyes caught him out. He was almost there, but he'd been spotted.

'That wily old wolf,' came a voice, whispering quietly to itself. 'He's better off out than in. Good luck to him.' It was the pike.

The key turned and MacDowell was out, skipping down to the harbour feeling full of himself.

It took him the rest of the morning to find out what had happened to his business colleagues. The ship was empty when he finally managed to get himself out there, and then it took him another half an hour to get back. By the time he'd caught up on the fast-moving events on Crampton Rock and knocked on the door of the old mill house, it was early afternoon.

\*

Back at the Hall, Victor was about to change MacDowell's water bowl. Mrs Carelli couldn't stand going up there any more; she'd had enough. She wanted rid of him. And whether she liked it or not, she already was.

Victor inspected the damage. The door and the wall next to it were completely destroyed. The room smelled of animal, the whole place was filthy, and it was also empty.

'Violet, come quickly!' shouted Victor. 'MacDowell is out of his room. He's in the house!'

But by now Mac was locked in a serious argument with his trader friends.

'You brought us here under false pretences,' said Beale. 'All you did was put our lives at risk. Even now, Mister Grimble lies in 'is bed with a fever. You promised us much,

MacDowell, and you have delivered nothin'.'

'Yer know what, I don't believe yer for a minute. You've found that gold. I know yer have. If Grimble made his way through those mines, he saw it with his own eyes. You're hidin' him from me because he can't lie to my face, I know it. I wants me money.'

'Mister Nook, would you remove this man please?' asked Beale.

'What are yer doin' movin' to the Rock, if there ain't nothin' 'ere?'

yelled Mac, who was now struggling with Mr
Nook. He dug his feet into the floor, held on
to the doorframe, and Nook had to peel his
fingers away before he slammed the door
shut.

MacDowell landed on his back in the
street. His shouting had already caused a stir
of onlookers. He got up and screamed
through the lock. 'I'll make yer regret this,
yer bunch o' bodgin' buccaneers!' With
nothing left to say, he escaped over the
moor to calm his nerves.

The old mill house was a
stone's throw from the Darkling
home, and the children had
watched through the tattered
lace curtains as the
argument took place.
Annabelle took the lead, and

they headed off to find Stanley and Daisy
and pass on the news.

As the daylight faded, thoughts of the
werewolf curse played on MacDowell's mind.
Soon he would be feeling the twinges and
aches that came with the onset of dusk, and
his body was wearing badly. Every day he
grew more exhausted, but every night the
fever of the wolf was more intense.

He couldn't take it much longer. If he
wasn't going to get his money, there was
something he must do to take his revenge.

When the sun had slipped behind the hills,
he sniffed out a trail that had been left by Mr
Darkling. It took him right to the very spot
where his four-legged friend had emerged
from the mines: a dangerous series of ledges
that stuck out from the rocks on the far
north-west corner of the island. Only an

animal such as a wolf
could take that leap.
And so he waited.

When the light was low, he felt it start all
over again. The aching limbs that he thought
couldn't take any more were shocked into
contortions that made him wince and whine.
And as he felt himself become the wolf once
more, the pain left him and his cry turned

into a howl. He felt, for that moment,
immensely strong again.

He prowled with his head down, scanning
the moor, then leaping on to the parapet and
padding his way through the dark, into
the mines he went. Deeper and deeper,
searching for the
scent of life.

Eventually, the smell of
humans poured through his
nostrils. He followed the trail,
deeper and deeper, until at
last he picked up the faint
CHINK … CHINK …
CHINK of hammers and

chisels against stone. And the lure of voices: three deep and dangerous voices.

He stared through the black ahead to the small flickers of candlelight in the distance. Now he could see them: Beale, Nook and Grimble, about to meet their end.

'We have to work out what to do with those kids,' said Nook as he worked away on the gold.

'Don't panic, Mister Nook,' said Beale. 'You worry too much. When we've established that the seam of gold runs right through these tunnels, the whole place will be up in smoke. Whilst we sit out in the ship drinking to our good fortune, this island's problems will be lost in the crumbling dust.'

Just then, Grimble noticed something from the corner of his eye: a movement in the dark. He looked across. One demonic yellow eye stared at him.

'Something's there,' he cried. 'Look. In the dark, up ahead.'

But they didn't need to look too hard. The wolf walked into the light, circling them. Beale and Nook were frozen, but Grimble's

fever had been growing worse and he dropped to his knees. He didn't know what was happening to him, but a ripping pain shot through his body like a surge of hot metal through his skin.

He began to cry out. His limbs lengthened. His back curved outwards, cracking as it went, echoing through the tunnels. A wave of strength washed over him, and in his fully-formed wolf shape he felt revitalized.

Beale and Nook watched in terror as the two wolves circled each other then pounced, locking heads like battling stags. They tore greedily at one another, baring white fangs that pierced like needles. Blood began to spill, dropping into the seawater that had begun to run around their feet.

Rocks and stones rumbled and fell as the

hulking shapes hurled each other
from wall to wall. Cracks
rippled through the narrow
gaps and dust clouded up
into the air.

It seemed to go on for hours:
tearing and clawing and
heaving, gasping and
snorting.
In a last attempt to
win the battle, the
pair of them
exploded into

furious rage. Steam billowed from their
nostrils as they ploughed into each other
mercilessly. Finally, with blood and saliva
trailing from their mouths, they both
dropped dead into the water that had
collected around them.

As their lives expired, the last spark of
their souls left their bodies like dancing
firelights and rattled through the tunnels,
burning themselves out.

The Rock was at last free from the curse of
the werewolf … and old MacDowell was
relieved of his troubles for ever.

·Milk· and Biscuits

The Darkling children were explaining what they had seen to Stanley and Daisy.

'We'd better get down there and at least find out what's been happening,' insisted Daisy.

MacDowell had been missing from his room for almost twenty-four hours now and they needed some answers.

It was a sunny afternoon. The Secret-Keepers Alliance marched across the village to the Darkling place. Within five minutes, all of them were puffing and blowing, heaving up the heavy flagstone that gave access to the tunnels.

Annabelle handed out the candle-ends they had 'borrowed' from Victor at the candle shop. Daisy held out a flame and delivered a spark of life to each one.

They nodded to each other and down they went: Stanley first, then Annabelle, and Daisy lowered the little ones into Stanley's arms before following on.

Through the darkened depths they trod, taking the short walk to where the mill house stood above them.

'Oh my goodness!' cried Annabelle.

Daisy joined in. 'I don't believe it,' she

squealed, her hands up to her mouth.

'I knew it,' said Stanley.

For now the mines were empty of buccaneers, but the hole they had made was huge, a vast cavern revealing more and more seams of shining gold.

'This place will collapse if they do much more,' said Stanley. 'We're going to have to let everyone know and get them away from here.'

Berkeley and Olive had spotted the bodies of the wolves, locked together in a final clinch of death.

Between them they worked out what must have happened. 'Poor old Mac,' said Daisy. 'I know he caused us problems, but you wouldn't wish that on anyone, would you?'

'There's less meat to buy now, Stanley,' said Berkeley.

'I guess you're right,' sighed Stanley. 'I guess you're right.' He got down on his knees and pulled the bodies into what looked like a more comfortable pose.

'What now?' he added, standing up.

'We need a milk and biscuits assembly,' insisted Daisy. 'Good home baking will settle our minds before we tell the Rock what has been happening.'

She was right: even the Darkling children were warming to biscuits. Who couldn't love Mrs Carelli's baking?

\*

They gathered at dusk in Stanley's room, seated neatly in their usual circle. They always sat in the same places: Stanley under the window, with Daisy to his left by the door and Annabelle opposite him, then Olive and Berkeley on his right.

'Good. Shall we begin?' asked Daisy.

There was obviously something Annabelle needed to say. She had avoided broaching the subject, but things had grown desperate.

'Would you like to begin, Annie?' said Stanley.

'Yes, please!' Annabelle answered nervously. 'There's something I need to let you know.'

'Do go on,' begged Daisy. 'That's why we're here.'

'Well … you might laugh!' she said with a straight face.

This was enough to set Berkeley off, and this in turn sent Olive into a fit of belly giggles.

'We won't laugh,' said Stanley, glaring at the young ones. 'We promise.'

'It's the pike,' Annabelle began. 'The one in

the glass case in the hallway.'

Everyone was silent. Stanley stared at the young ones, expecting more giggles, but no, they were deadly serious.

'He spoke to me. He said that Stanley had taken to not listening to his advice any more and that he very much wanted to pass him some information. It's stupid, I know. I wasn't sure if I'd only imagined it. But it's happened again since.'

'He spoke to us too,' said Berkeley and Olive at the same time. They looked at each other and then back at everybody else. 'We thought we were dreaming.'

'Don't worry, Annie,' said Stanley. 'I know for sure that the pike on the wall speaks. I've taken help from him in the past. The last time I spoke with him, I was growing tired of his riddles. One thing's for sure: if he's desperate to tell us something, we must listen.'

'To the pike, everybody!' said Daisy. As they got to their feet, Berkeley sent the milk jug flying.

'BERKELEY!'

11

To the Pike

'Ahh, the famous five,' grinned the pike, as the children gathered around the glass case in the gloominess of the hallway. They stared at him expectantly, waiting for him to speak. He took his time before he began, clearing his throat. 'Ahem ...'

'Get on with it,' said Stanley. 'He does like the sound of his own voice, you know,' he

said, turning to the others.

They giggled nervously.

'Firstly,' said the pike, 'I would like Stanley to assure me of something. Tell me that you still have the map that brought you to the smugglers' mine, my dear boy.'

'Of course,' laughed Stanley. 'It's one of my most important possessions. It lies in the silver casket in my room, behind the false panel. Everything is in place, just as it should be! Why do you ask?'

'Let me explain,' the pike continued, clearing his throat again. 'In the past, Stanley, I have let you work out the answers for yourself. But now the risk is much greater and time is of the essence.

'Take yourselves out on to the moor and build a small fire. Put the ancient map in the middle and make sure it burns well. It must burn right through the night. Don't worry about losing it: the map has no real purpose any more, except for that which I am about to explain. In the morning, gather the ashes from the fire while they are still hot. Take a small amount each, and scatter them across the moor above the mines.'

'And then what?' asked Annabelle and

Daisy at the same time.

'Sometimes, my dears, the only thing you can do is sit and wait. You will have played your part, and that is enough. Just make sure

you stay out of the way!'

And that was all he would say. The children waited, just to be sure.

'What's your name?' asked Berkeley.

But the pike was already asleep, dreaming of a warm swim with the sunlight piercing through the surface of the water.

Berkeley tapped on the glass, leaving greasy finger marks.

'Come on,' said Stanley. 'We may as well get started.' He ran to his room and uncovered the secret panel that held the shining silver casket, took it out from its home and dusted it down.

By now the night was black and as far as the Rock was concerned, werewolf status was on high alert. The alliance would have to be

extra careful to avoid the look-outs, especially since they were building a fire.

A small procession of silky black silhouettes filed its way out on to the moor through the back garden of Candlestick Hall. Each member of the alliance carried a small supply of wooden planks and sticks gathered from outside the house. When they decided they'd reached the right spot, they grouped together in the darkness.

And then, over the black plain of the rolling hills, a small orangey-yellow spark of life appeared, seemingly out of nowhere. It grew larger and larger until soon it was a burning ball of fire with orange cinders crackling from its belly and spiralling upwards into the air.

Stanley rolled the ragged pieces of the map around a dried-up old twig and inserted it carefully into the centre, like he'd seen Mrs Carelli do with the poker.

He held it there and watched the age-old map disintegrate into nothing, shrivelling into black wispy embers that floated above him. Somehow what he was doing didn't feel right, but he believed in the pike, who'd never let him down or told him an untruth.

The children stayed a while and fed the fire's hungry red mouth until its centre roared

a fierce white hot, so fierce that by morning it would still be scorching to the touch.

And then the final act would be carried out under the sunlight of the following day.

An unexpected turn

As morning arrived, Daisy looked out from her room in the lighthouse. She could see Stanley's shape at his window. And then she looked across the moor and spotted a fine trail of smoke from the last living moments of the fire.

They would have to be there promptly: if someone else came across it they might stamp it out and scatter the ashes into the grass. Daisy realized that those embers were more valuable now than the map had ever been.

The alliance had arranged an early meet, and they were all there promptly – apart from Olive, who'd left the house without her doll and was made to return on her own.

'I must have it,' she'd wailed.

'The plan won't work if she isn't there. She's part of the alliance!' insisted Stanley. And soon she was back, headless doll clutched tightly.

A pile of grey ash lay at their feet. Berkeley took a stick and opened it up. Stanley took the stick gently from Berkeley and separated the ashes to cool them. A gentle breeze blew across the moor.

Within a few minutes they were each able to take a handful of the grey dust.

'It doesn't look like it would make any difference to anything,' said Annabelle, staring into her hands.

'We must trust the pike,' said Stanley. He sent everyone to different parts of the moor, and each in turn spread out their own share.

Stanley knew that Olive and Berkeley would expect something to come about immediately. They'd pester him until he told them what was going to happen and so far he

didn't have a clue. So he announced that he was going back to bed for an hour and that they should meet up in the afternoon. (Perhaps by then something might have taken place.)

This seemed like the perfect idea until he was back indoors and Mrs Carelli stood waiting, wanting to know who was lighting fires on the moor, what the children were doing out there at the crack of dawn and where on earth old MacDowell was, he'd been missing for days.

'Erm …' began Stanley.

'Erm indeed,' she started, then hurled punishing words and sentences at him until his head ached and he was tempted to slip back out through the door.

'No you don't,' she called out. 'You can clean this hearth out and fetch in some fresh

logs, seeing as you're in the mood for fires.'
She lunged the dustpan and brush into his
arms and left the room.

Victor peered over his glasses at Stanley.
'Looks like you're in trouble again,' he
chortled.

When his chores were complete and he'd
eaten a plateful, Stanley was ready for the

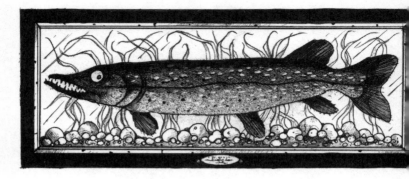

Darklings again. Actually, he wasn't. But he was eager to see if he could find out what was happening.

He sneaked a chat with the pike before he left.

'Ahh, Stanley, friend of the Rock. You do a good job when you set your mind to it. Well done. But steer clear of the mines!'

Stanley was pleased with himself: he appreciated a compliment from someone as cynical as the pike.

But it wasn't enough to make him leave well alone; he had to know what was happening.

'Stanley would not be Stanley if he wasn't in the thick of the action,' mumbled the pike.

When Stanley opened the front door of the Hall, Daisy and the Darklings were right outside.

'There's a lot of noise down in the mines, Stanley,' said Annabelle. 'We could hear it from the basement. But it's not digging, it's something different. Movements of some kind!'

'Why were you in the basement? You haven't been—'

He was cut short by Annabelle. 'Stanley, calm down, we haven't done a thing.'

'All right,' he said. 'Let's take a look. Where are your mother and father?'

'We told them to take a walk across the moor. We watched them walk through the village and talk to people. Everyone thinks

Father is our uncle, because he looks
so different.'

'Perfect,' said Daisy. 'Let's go.'

'But the pike warned us to stay away,' said
Berkeley, tugging on Stanley's shirt.

'I just want to take a look,' said Stanley.

'That's all.'

But just taking a look turned into
something else, something that changed
everything for ever.

The flagstone-lifting episode wasn't
getting any easier: if anything, it seemed
heavier. Down they went, down the cold,
black pathway into the unknown. The tide
was right back and for now they were safe
from danger. Or, at least, the kind of danger
that high tide brought to the tunnels.

But other problems soon surfaced. They

couldn't hear the traders, there was no hammering of chisels … but there was something else. Trails of wire adorned the walls and floors.

Stanley inspected them closely.

'Oh no. Fuse wire!' he gasped, a lump forming in his throat.

'What's "fyoose wayer"?' asked Berkeley.

Stanley was distracted and didn't answer. He followed the course of the wire through the tunnel, the others behind him.

The wire ended at a box. Explosives. Daisy held up her candle and shone a faint light down the tunnel. More wire, more boxes.

'Stop, don't panic,' said Stanley, panicking!

'We need to put out these candles,' Daisy urged. 'If we let a spark touch that wire, we'll all go up in smoke and the Rock will

follow on behind us.'

'But we can't see without the candles,' Stanley objected.

'Put them out,' said Annabelle. 'We can see in the dark. Hold on to one of us.'

For the moment there was no sign of Beale and Nook, but something was stirring in the darkness. If only they could see more clearly, thought Stanley. Somehow the mines themselves seemed to be alive, shifting and whispering!

They were coming to a cavern. Candles were glued to the walls, glowing softly.

Only then did the full horror of what was about to happen unveil itself to them.

'Look,' said Stanley. 'The walls really *are* moving.'

And the alliance stared wide-eyed as they saw what was happening.

The magic had begun to work. The ashes of the map had seeped into the earth and the very Rock had started to come to life.

Nearby, a skeletal pirate hand twitched until the movement rippled along the length of its stone-encrusted arms and legs.

Life began to pour into every bit of the twisting mines and would not stop until every ancient limb of each long-dead pirate was awake.

Just ahead, a fully-formed skeletal buccaneer dropped from the curved ceiling and landed on his feet. Then another, and another and another.

It was only now that Stanley understood the pike's instructions to stay well away. But perhaps it was a little late!

Bones clicked and drummed in time with each other. A sea of grinning faces looked back at the children, shields and swords raised. The ancient pirates were joined in their purpose to protect the Rock and all they could see were intruders.

Stanley chose the nearest hole and hurled everyone down it. 'Run!' he screamed at Berkeley.

They thundered onward through the mines, the buccaneers chasing them through the darkness. But the more they ran, the more the pirates' numbers gathered behind them as one by one the skeletal protectors awoke.

Stanley took a sneaky glimpse behind him. By now there must be hundreds.

The only advantage the children held was that they were small and they flew through the tiny spaces like little rockets – all except for Annabelle, whose height meant she kept banging her head.

Stanley pushed them on, but the children were so exhausted they could barely keep going.

The gathering force behind them was so large that its noise became deafening.

Stanley was thinking quickly

as he ran, and threw his directions towards
the front.

'Follow the fuse wire, Berkeley.'

Berkeley puffed and blew; he was running
out of steam. The musical sound of the
skeletons' hollow bones echoed in the
children's ears.

But at last they could hear the sounds that
told Stanley he was where he wanted to be.

'Hear those voices, Berkeley?'

'Yeah,' Berkeley replied, gasping.

'That's what we're heading for.'

Olive was flagging, slowing right down
until the others were almost tripping over
her. Stanley put his hands around her waist
and hoisted her up, carrying her along.

'Keep going!' he roared.

Only seconds later, the children spilled out
into a big cave and fell on top of one
another, gasping for air. But Stanley looked
up and could see what he
had wanted to find: Beale
and Nook, laying more
fuse wire.

'It's those pesky kids
again. You're a little late,'
grinned Mr
Nook.

'Really?' said Stanley. 'That's a shame. I wanted you to meet your neighbours.'

Right there and then the hordes of warriors filed out of the narrow tunnels, fixing their eyes upon the two villains. Nook and Beale stared back in sheer panic. For a

second everyone was still.

The alliance looked to Stanley.

Mr Nook held his shotgun in both hands, shaking violently. Mr Beale was equally dumbfounded and seemed unable to move.

Swords were raised, shields were primed, and the commotion began.

Stanley had to get his gang out of there.

As the treasure thieves were confronted by its protectors, Stanley pulled the children on to all fours and they sneaked away unnoticed. Through a crowd of bony legs they filed in line to the nearest escape hole.

Down they went into the darkness, up to their elbows and thighs in water, until they reached a pinprick of light that led them to an empty space where more candles were slowly burning out. And as they went they listened to the clattering of swords and shields as Beale and Nook fought for their lives.

The battle would be begun and finished, like so many others had been, in the depths of the smugglers' mine.

In a short while they were back in the basement. Water had started to wash through the mines, and the dynamite would now prove to be useless as it swam around in the drink.

As they spilled out on to the rough grass at the back of the Darkling house Mr and Mrs Darkling appeared, back from one of their walks with Steadman.

'Get down,' said Stanley, and they hunched into a corner as the pair sauntered by, talking and smiling. The Darkling children had been so wrapped up in recent events that they had neglected to notice how much happier things had become at home: Mrs Darkling was more cheerful than she had ever been, and Mr Darkling was somehow a milder-mannered, more pleasant form of his old self.

Steadman wagged his broad tail, licked Stanley's face and then carried on behind Mr and Mrs Darkling.

Eventually they made it back to Candlestick Hall.

Mr and Mrs Carelli stood at the door as the sand-caked, sodden figures of the Secret-Keepers Alliance wandered towards them.

Stanley expected Mrs Carelli to explode. She had probably just mopped the floor, or cleaned the hallway. But with an expression that almost said, 'I give in', she greeted them in turn and watched them tread mud

through the house.

In a short while the alliance were standing under the glass case, reporting the fantastical episode to the pike.

'Who would have believed it?' laughed Stanley. 'Saved by pirates after all!'

'A happy ending?' said Daisy, turning to Annabelle and the twins.

'Well, about as happy as it could get on the Rock!' said Olive and Berkeley at the same time.

'What will become of the skeletal buccaneers?' quizzed Stanley.

'Oh, don't worry. As quickly as they awoke, they'll return to their sleep,' the pike assured them.

'And if anyone else tries to take the gold?' asked Daisy.

'Good luck to them! They won't get very

far,' the pike replied. 'Now, can I rest? I don't seem to have slept soundly in such a long time. Not since Stanley first arrived!'

'I'm sure you can sleep,' said Stanley. 'The Rock is at peace.' He looked out through the open window on to the harbour as the moonlight began to wash across the streets and houses.

In a short while the pike was indeed asleep. He slept comfortably at first, but then he began to twitch. His heart beat a little faster. Fast enough to wake him in wonder. He stared with an open eye into

the blackness of the corridor. And he was
sure, just for a moment, that something was
about to disturb him!

Scribbles from the

# Something Wickedly Weird

sketchbook

Chris Mould

Chris Mould went to art school at the age of sixteen. During this time, he did various jobs, from delivering papers to washing up and cooking in a kitchen. He has won the Nottingham Children's Book Award and been commended for the Sheffield. He loves his work and likes to write and draw the kind of books that he would have liked to have on his shelf as a boy. He is married with two children and lives in Yorkshire.

**Crampton Rock** seems the perfect place to spend a long summer holiday. But there's always something to go and spoil it all, isn't there?

Why are all the **dogs three-legged?**
Is there really a **werewolf** on the loose?
And what do the *pirates* want with Stanley Buggles...?

All looks crisp and cosy in **Crampton Rock** as Stanley Buggles settles down for the winter. But something wicked has blown in with the wind.

What is the **headless ghost** of Admiral Swift desperate to tell Stanley?

And who are the **deadly pirates**, marching through the oncoming blizzard ...?

Up ahead, the shape of **Crampton Rock** grows clear through the misty glass of a hundred telescopes. The black pirate swarm moves ever closer for the final battle.

What has awoken the **skeletons** from their slumber? And how can Stanley Buggles *escape* from their deadly grip ...?

Something Wickedly Weird

THE SILVER CASKET

The island of **Crampton Rock** has emerged from **pirate battle**. But something far more sinister is on the move...

What claim does the **Darkling family** have on Stanley Buggles' home?

And do the Darkling twins really keep a **two-headed snake** as a pet?

Something Wickedly Weird
THE DARKLING CURSE

CHRIS MOULD